'In this excoriating indictment of the white supremacy underpinning the office space, Natasha Brown shows us the triple bind under which Black British women live. How can there be wholeness in a society that demands so often that Black women melt parts of themselves down so that the machinery can shape them anew? I have scarcely read a work of fiction that confronts me so clearly and viscerally with the nature of injustice in our contemporary moment. This is an important work from a writer I hope we'll be hearing from for a long, long time'

Kayo Chingonyi

'This marvel of a novel manages to say all there is to say about Britain today in the most precise, poetic prose and within the story of one complicated, compelling woman. Formally thrilling, politically captivating, endlessly absorbing . . . I will never forget where I was when I read it, how I felt at the start of it and by the end – it takes you on a complete carousel of a life lived both in dread and in defiance. Superb'

Sabrina Mahfouz

'*Assembly* feels thrillingly like the fictional companion to Jamaica Kincaid's non-fiction masterpiece *A Small Place*; where *A Small Place* dissected British imperialism and coloniality as manifested in Antigua, Brown turns that keen, forensic gaze back to England's own green and not so pleasant land, filleting through its mores and pulling back its veneer of civility with the steady, sure hand of a surgeon. A book like a finely honed scalpel – marking a new and electrifying dawn for the essay novel'

Elaine Castillo

'A piercing cautionary tale about the costs of assimilating into a society still in denial about its colonial past. Brown writes with the deftness and insight of a poet'

Mary Jean Chan

'Deft, essential and a novel of poetic consideration, *Assembly* holds (the Black British) identity in its hands, examining it until it becomes both truer and stranger – a question more than an answer. I nodded, I *mhmmed*, I sighed (and laughed knowingly, bitterly)'

Rachel Long

'As utterly, urgently brilliant as everyone has said. A needle driven directly into the sclerotic heart of contemporary Britain. Beautiful proof that you don't need to write a long book, just a good book'

Rebecca Tamás

'Bold, elegant and all the more powerful for its brevity, *Assembly* captures the sickening weightlessness that a Black British woman, who has been obedient to and complicit with the capitalist system, experiences as she makes life-changing decisions under the pressure of the hegemony'

Paul Mendez

'*Assembly* is brilliant. Natasha Brown's ability to slide between the tiniest, most telling detail and the edifice of history, the assemblage of so many lives in so many times and places, is as breathtakingly graceful as it is mercilessly true'

Olivia Sudjic

'A short but exceptionally powerful novel from a gifted new writer'

Bookseller, Editor's Choice

'A stunning achievement of compressed narrative and fearless articulation'

Publishers Weekly

ABOUT THE AUTHOR

Natasha Brown has spent a decade working in financial services, after studying Maths at Cambridge University. *Assembly* is her first novel.

PENGUIN BOOKS

Assembly

'Slim in the hand, but its impact is massive; it strikes me as the kind of book that sits on the fault line between a before and an after. I could use words like "elegant" and "brilliantly judged", and literary antecedents such as Katherine Mansfield/Toni Morrison/Claudia Rankine. But it's simpler than that. I'm full of the hope, on reading it, that this is the kind of book that doesn't just mark the moment things change, but also makes that change possible'
Ali Smith

'Brilliantly sharp and curiously Alice-like . . . Her indictment is forensic, clear, elegant . . . a prose-polished looking glass held up to her not-so-post-colonial nation. Only one puzzle remains unsolved: how a novel so slight can bear such weight'
The Times Literary Supplement

'*Assembly* fulfils, with exquisite precision, Virginia Woolf's exhortation to "record the atoms as they fall upon the mind in the order in which they fall" . . . [It] calls to mind Frantz Fanon's work on the psychic ruptures caused by the experience of being colonized, or W. E. B. Du Bois's idea of double consciousness . . . Brown nudges us towards an expression of the inexpressible – towards feeling rather than thought – as if we are navigating the collapsing boundaries between the narrator's consciousness and our own'

Guardian

'*Assembly* expertly draws out the difficulties of assembling a coherent self in the face of myriad structural oppressions. Casting a wry look at faded aristocrats, financial insiders and smug liberals, Natasha Brown takes the conventional tics of the English novel – the repressed emotion and clipped speech – and drains away the nostalgia. What's left is something hard and true'

Will Harris

'*Assembly* is extraordinary, each word weighed, each detail meticulously crafted . . . Brown is mercilessly clear-eyed in her delineation of how British culture is also "assembled" – its history whitewashed and arguing against it near-impossible when "the only tool of expression is the language of this place". Yet she wields that language like a weapon and hits her mark again and again with devastating elegance'

The Times

'This is a heartbreaking novel that offers glimmers of hope with its bold vision for new modes of storytelling . . . Brown's voice is entirely her own – and *Assembly* is a wry, explosive debut from a coruscating new talent'

i

'Brown gets straight to the point. With delivery as crisp as biting into an apple, she short-circuits expectation . . . This is [the narrator's] story, and she will tell it how she wishes, unpicking convention and form. Like *The Driver's Seat* by Muriel Spark, it's thrilling to see a protagonist opting out and going her own way'

Scotsman

'This powerful short novel suggests meaningful discussion of race is all but impossible if imperialism's historical violence remains taboo'

Daily Mail

'Coiled and charged, a small shockwave . . . Sometimes you come across a short novel of such compressed intensity that you wonder why anyone would bother reading longer narratives . . . *Assembly* casts a huge shadow'

Moneycontrol

'An achievement that will leave you wondering just how it's possible that this is only the author's very first work. It may be taut at only 112 pages, but Brown packs so much commentary and insight inside of every single sentence that you still feel like you're getting *much* more than your money's worth'

Shondaland

Assembly

Natasha Brown

PENGUIN BOOKS

PENGUIN BOOKS

UK | USA | Canada | Ireland | Australia
India | New Zealand | South Africa

Penguin Books is part of the Penguin Random House
group of companies whose addresses can be found at
global.penguinrandomhouse.com.

First published by Hamish Hamilton 2021
Published in Penguin Books 2022
001

Printed and bound in Great Britain by Clays Ltd, Elcograf S.p.A.

The authorized representative in the EEA is
Penguin Random House Ireland,
Morrison Chambers, 32 Nassau Street,
Dublin D02 YH68

A CIP catalogue record for this book is
available from the British Library

ISBN: 978–0–241–99266–1

www.greenpenguin.co.uk

This too is meaningless,
a chasing after the wind.

Alright

You have to stop this, she said.

Stop what, he said, we're not doing anything. She wanted to correct him. There was no we. There was he the subject and her the object, but he just told her look, there's no point getting worked up over nothing.

.

She often sat in the end cubicle of the ladies' room and stared at the door. She'd sit for an entire lunch break, sometimes, waiting either to shit or to cry or to muster enough resolve to go back to her desk.

He could see her at her desk from his office and regularly dialled her extension to comment on what he saw (and what he made of it): her hair (wild), her skin (exotic), her blouse (barely containing those breasts).

Over the phone, he instructed her to do little things. This humiliated her more than the bigger things that eventually followed. Still, she held her stapler up high as directed. Drank her entire glass of water in one go. Spat out her chewing gum into her hand.

•

She had gone to lunch with her colleagues. They were six men of varying ages, sizes and temperaments. They ordered four plates of the beef nigiri and, during the meal, occasionally referenced her situation via vague innuendo and accusatory observations.

One of the older ones, fat with a thick greying beard around his thin pink lips, put down his fork to talk straight. He began slowly: He knows she's not one to take advantage of it. He knows that, he knows. There, he paused for effect and to savour the thrill of telling the girl how things were. But – but now, she must admit, she had an advantage over him and the others at the table. She could admit that, couldn't she.

He smiled wide, opened his arms wide and leaned back. The other five looked at her, some nodding. He picked up his fork again and shoved more raw meat into his mouth.

•

His office was glass on three sides. Rows of desks stretched out to the right and left, a spectators' gallery. She had centre stage. He sat talking to her, quite animated.

He hoped she would show some maturity, he said, some appreciation. He was getting up from his chair, walking towards her, brushing against her though the office was large and he had plenty of space. She should think of the big picture and her future and what his word means around here. He said this as he opened the office door.

·

It was nothing. She thought this now, as she thought it each morning. She buttoned up her shirt and thought it, then pushed small studs into her ears. She thought it as she pulled her hair back into a neat bun, left her face bare, smoothed down her stiff, grey pencil skirt.

She thought it as she ate, even as she forgot how to taste or swallow. She tried to chew. It was nothing. She barked that she was fine, then softened, looked around the living room. Asked her mother how her day had been.

·

Dinner after work, she'd agreed to it. Outside the restaurant, before they went in, he grabbed her shoulders and pressed his open mouth on to her face.

She watched his eyelids quiver shut as his slow tongue pushed and poked at hers. She pictured her body, limbs folded, packed away in a box. He stepped back, smiled, laughed a bit, looked down at her. He touched her arm, then her fingers, and then her face. It's alright, he told her. It's alright, it's alright.

What It's Like

No, but originally. Like your parents, where they're from. Africa, right?

Here's the thing. I've been here five years. My wife –
seven, eight. We've been working, we've been paying
our taxes. We cheer for England in the World Cup!
So when the government told us to register; told us
to download this app and pay to register, it hurt.
This is our home. We felt unwelcome. It's like if they
said to you: Go back to Africa. Imagine if they told
you: no-no, you're not a real Brit, go back to Africa.
That's what it's like.

I mean it's – well, you know. Of course you do, you
understand. You can understand it in a way the
English don't.

After the Digestif, He Gets Going

She understood the anger of a man who himself understood in his flesh and bones and blood and skin that he was meant to be at the head of a great, hulking giant upon whom the sun never set. Because it was night, now, and he was drunk. He felt very small, perhaps only a mouth. A lip or a tooth or a rough, inflamed bud on a dry white tongue slick with phlegm at the back, near the throat. The throat of a man with a sagging gut and thinning hair cropped short. So, when that mouth opened up and coughed its vitriol at her, making some at the table a little uncomfortable, she understood the source of its anger, despite being the target. She waited for the buzz of her phone to excuse her and – in the meantime – quietly, politely, she understood him.

ASSEMBLY

It's a story. There are challenges. There's hard work, pulling up laces, rolling up shirtsleeves, and forcing yourself. Up. Overcoming, transcending, et cetera. You've heard it before. It's not my life, but it's illuminated two metres tall behind me and I'm speaking it into the soft, malleable faces tilted forwards on uniformed shoulders. I recite my old lines like new secrets. Click to the next slide. Giant, diverse, smiling faces in grey suits point at charts, shake hands and wave behind me. The projector whirrs and their smiles morph into the bank's roaring logo. Time to wrap up. I look out around the rows of schoolgirls. Thank them for listening, before taking questions.

One asks if I live in a mansion.

It was a hit, the programme coordinator tells me and the head teacher nods a frazzled bob of greying hair. Her tense lips part, flashing coffee-yellow teeth. We're walking round and down a small back stairway and I'm gagging on the warm air, that boiled-veg school smell. The head teacher thanks me for coming, says the girls were all inspired. Shrieks, laughter and a booming, melodic chatter echo around us as the students splash out of the assembly hall and into concrete corridors. Simply inspirational, she says.

Back at the office, Lou's not in yet. He rarely shows up before eleven. As if each morning, fresh mediocrity slides out of the ocean, slimes its way over mossy rocks and sand, then sprouts skittering appendages that stretch and morph and twist into limbs as it forges on inland until finally, fully formed, *Lou!* strolls into the lobby on two flat feet in shined shoes. Shining, tapping, waiting for the lift to our floor. Nodding to the Beats buds in his ears. He's never roped in to all this. I do these talks – schools and universities, women's panels, recruiting fairs – every few weeks. It's an expectation of the job. The diversity must be seen. How many women and girls have I lied to? How many have seen my grinning face advocating for this or that firm, or this industry, or that university, this life? Such questions aren't constructive. I need to catch up on the morning's lost hours.

For much of my own childhood, I lived next to a cemetery. Through the front windows, I'd watch funeral processions snake along the road: black horses followed by black hearses followed by regular cars in different colours. Sometimes a man marched in front with a top hat and cane. Then the people: getting out of the cars and the hearses and gathering themselves, carrying wreaths, carrying hats. Carrying coffins, too, I guess. I don't remember seeing that. They'd gather by the mounds of fresh-dug dirt and wait around, wreaths piled neat beside them, or they'd just stand there holding flowers. Or holding each other. Little faraway creatures, clinging together for comfort. I watched from above.

Last year, I bought the top floor of a Georgian conversion in an up-and-coming area. The other two flats are each rented out by youngish, anxious couples. A tense argument over music volumes escalates nightly between them.

The improbably named Adam and Evie have the ground floor. When we met in the stairwell, Evie introduced herself first, as Adam's girlfriend. She brushed wispy strands of blonde hair back from her forehead and told me she worked in publishing. When the music's too loud, she'll knock at the flat above and implore them to *please*, turn it *down*. Just a *tad*. Her cut-glass exasperation sends shards right up through my own floor.

The other couple is sullen and reclusive. They rarely speak, though I've heard their enthusiastic wailing over 90s bangers. They're both pretty; brunettes with sharp features and small feet. Two pairs of tiny, muddy football boots lie drying outside their front door every Thursday morning.

The familiar rhythms of our stacked lives have become a kind of closeness.

At work, I think of the flat as parents must pine when they see their kids' smiling faces framed and propped up amongst the papers and cups on their desks. My friend Rach – small, spoilt, energetic – waves away her own home in a leafy West London suburb. Says she wants a bigger house, a better boyfriend, more money! She wants all these things without shame or subtlety and I'm both fearful and admiring of her appetite. My own is gone. I've sunk too deep, pulled down further by a creeping, winding tightness around my limbs. Still, I hold my breath.

What else is there?

Generations of sacrifice; hard work and harder living. So much suffered, so much forfeited, so much – for this opportunity. For my life. And I've tried, tried living up to it. But after years of struggling, fighting against the current, I'm ready to slow my arms. Stop kicking. Breathe the water in. I'm exhausted. Perhaps it's time to end this story.

Ah – here's Lou.

Conversations

Yesterday, as I sat waiting in the bright reception area of the private oncologist's Harley Street office I had visited now three times, I experienced a detachment – not imagined; no, it was a tangible, physical phenomenon. Something had plucked within. An untethering of self from experience.

I quite liked going there. The receptionists – young, pretty, interchangeable – were polite, always. And welcomed me as though we were at a spa. The flowers that day were huge lilies with gaping petals and thick stems. Stamens, snipped clinically, left smudged red pollen on the white petals. You couldn't un-see O'Keeffe. Two of us were there, waiting. With the un-rushed certainty of time blocked out in Outlook playing out as intended. From a tufted ottoman beside the window, I looked out at the street below.

My mother was always telling me over the phone about people who had recently died. Reminding me of so-and-so. Oh, of course I knew her – remember she used to stop by with her niece (sweet girl, you two were friends). Yes, yes, her. Well, she died last week. Isn't it? Terrible. I wasn't sure why this conversational habit bothered me so much. It wasn't gossipy, there was no malice. In fact, these frequent reports felt propelled by an unspoken loss. An exhaustive proof that we, whatever it was that bound us all together within the first-person plural, were not surviving. I decided my complaint was primarily formal, the set-up and punchline structure she employed; making me remember knowing, invoking memories of a person, of a life, then unveiling the death. It induced a roller-coaster lurch within my solar plexus. Tinged with a guilty numbness as I considered the absurd luxury aesthetic of my company healthcare provisions. The screenings, pre-emptive tests and speedy follow-ups that sustained life. I knew that we, the children who remained, would do so with weakened bonds. No common country or culture linked us other than British (which could only be claimed hyphenated or else parenthesized by the origins of those whose deaths our mothers detailed over the phone). It was survival only in the sense that a meme survives. Generational persistence, without meaning or memory.

I'd told my boyfriend it was fine. I was fine. He didn't need to accompany me. Still, he insisted we at least meet somewhere after work for a drink. An outing to lift the spirits. Fine. It was a nice enough evening, unseasonably warm for September. We drank beer on the grass outside the old pub near Blackfriars station. And everything, I told him, was fine. False alarm. False words could feel true. He was easily convinced, accustomed to happy endings and painless resolution. Nothing to worry about, we clinked the necks of our bottles together.

'I know I've been distant,' he said, 'not myself.'

I looked at my legs, shining brown in the evening sun. We'd moved on from biopsies, consultations and assertions of relief to talking about his work; big, important things he was peripherally involved in at Whitehall.

'I don't think I've been good company of late,' he said.

The weekend before, he'd slept with his head pressed against my chest, curled up like a foetus. Monday morning, he'd wrapped his arms around me so tight that I stayed in bed for an extra while and stroked his hair. Until I had to leave for work.

'Sometimes, I just –' He stopped and picked at the label on his beer bottle. It looked damp and soft from condensation and he tore off little pieces at a time, balled them up between his finger and thumb and flicked the sticky globs into the grass. When we'd first dated, he would brandish his name to maître d's with a booming exuberance. I wondered whether that sense of self had been picked away, or whether his self were only a dinner jacket he put on and then took off again. Head tilted back, he glugged from the bottle. His Adam's apple bobbed as he swallowed and I imagined cool beer flowing down his throat, along the curve of his chest and sloshing into his belly.

We met at college, he liked to say. Though I barely knew him back then. He was already in third year when I matriculated. I didn't remember ever speaking to him, though I knew his face and name from student politics. No, he only noticed me in the years after, at events in the occasional intersection of our overlapping social circles. My own social capital had increased – infinitesimally, immeasurably – since my student days. Money, even the relatively modest amount I'd amassed, had transformed me. My style, my mannerisms, my lightly affected City vernacular, all intrigued him. He could see the person I was constructing. And he sensed opportunity. He'd read of Warren Wilhelm Jr's transformation to Bill de Blasio.

Accidentally-on-purpose, he bumped against me at a rooftop barbecue in a Stepney warehouse conversion. Laid the Hugh Grant charm on thick as we sipped warm, fruity Pimm's from Mason jars. Canary Wharf gleamed and ached, beautiful, behind him. He had seemed too much, then, as though he were caricaturing himself. Over the ensuing months and years, I began to appreciate the elastic nature of his personality. I watched him jostle and mess about with his close friends. Debating big ideas with bigger words and a brutal sense of group humour. They poked fun at one another mercilessly, then chortled: bent over, knee slapping, in a near-parodical show of mirth. After, in the back of a minicab, he'd greet the driver by name and navigate expertly from idle chit-chat to unlocking a life story. He asked thoughtful follow-ups and never interrupted. He was polite, yes, but not stuffy. He softened his accent. Said, 'Good night, man,' sincerely, punctuated with a clasped two-hand hand-shake, before climbing out of the car.

'This is nice,' he said finally, almost smiling. And it was. Tomorrow seemed further away. Though the upcoming weekend with his parents still loomed large; their anniversary party hosted at the family's country estate. What should have felt, if not casual, then at least pleasantly exciting, was instead rapidly materi-alizing into hard reality. I nodded, and he turned to face the cars lined up at the crossing.

'I've been – I mean my ex.' He paused, then started again. 'My ex has been texting. She got a puppy.'

A puppy? I repeated, turning the syllables over. His ex would be at the anniversary, too, I knew. She was a childhood friend, virtually a part of the family, as his mother had phrased it. They'd grown up together frolicking across the English countryside like Colin and Mary Lennox. Looking at him, crouched there on the grass, with his cheeks and watery eyes contorted into an approximation of stoicism – I felt a curiosity, I wanted to know.

'Forget it,' he said. 'I shouldn't have mentioned the puppy.'

Our second bottles were empty. The background chatter had swelled to a buzz of only occasionally dissonant rhubarb, rhubarb, rhubarb. I asked to see the puppy, if he had a picture. He set down his bottle and stared at me for a while.

'Just forget about the puppy,' he said.

We took the District Line back to Putney. The declining sun smouldered behind chimneyed rooftops as we walked along quiet roads from the station to his house. Reading before bed, he smiled sideways over his Kindle at me. Later, as he slept, I watched his chest sink and swell. Heard his occasional, wheezing snores. He'd thrown off the bed sheet and lay on his back in a cherubic pose: left foot against right knee, right arm bent around his head, fingers spread soft on the pillow. Cock pink against his thigh. Gravity smoothed his forehead and cheeks and I recognized the boy-ish, pouting face from his driving licence.

Did I prefer this to sleeping alone?

My neighbours' lives were tangled up in their partners. They'd cleaved from their parents and unto each other, sharing bills, food, rent. I did not imagine they could easily separate. We had no such obligations. But we still visited galleries, watched plays, attended parties, hosted parties, travelled, cooked, together. We said *we*. This seemed a necessary aspect of life, like work. Or exercise.

'It's the principle,' Rach had told me, earlier that day. 'Fuck the sexism – harness it!'

Rach was adamant that her entanglement with one of the firm's global department heads was in fact her prerogative: to reclaim and subvert the narrative of workplace harassment. They were getting serious. Moving from formal praxis to something resembling mundane, genuine emotion. Living together. It was both simpler and more complex than my own relationship.

We had our usual table at the mezzanine coffee point above the office lobby. Rach's nails, peachy-manicured as always, tip-tapped against her almond latte. We'd slipped from co-workers to friends over the last year as her father recovered from cancer and my grandmother died of it. She was a Home Counties, Kate-loving, Jaeger-shopping, *Lean In*-feminist who arranged animal-welfare fundraisers at the weekends and bought handmade earrings from Etsy. She once called me in tears from the Hermès store. It's all too beautiful, she'd sobbed in halting syllables as the shop assistant packaged her scarves.

'Victimhood is a choice,' Rach said. Part opinion, part mantra. She insisted on continual improvement: evolution, learning, growth, smashing through all ceilings at all costs. She said there's a new victim every day. Didn't my MD just get axed for fucking around with that intern in Legal? She shook her head at such reckless, stupid hubris. This was how our conversations invariably went.

Still, Rach understood – even relished – the cut-throat nature of this place. And so, the coffee breaks, the drinks, the brunches, they continued. We were close, we were friends. We said it with post-postmodern earnestness: best friends. We made lists, reviewed our five-year plans and crunched out the Teflon-lined stomachs necessary for execution. There was a fundamental aspect of myself – un-storied and direct. The ugly machinery that grinds beneath all achievement. Only with Rach did I acknowledge that level.

'Who will they promote, do you think? To replace him.' She leaned back to consider her own question. Then lobbed a few names my way, chuckling as she evaluated Lou's chances.

'Or maybe they'll go for a woman,' she said, laying out each hand in turn, palm up. 'A woman harmed, another rewarded – sounds legit!'

She laughed, brushing her hands together. Despite the cynicism, I knew it got to her. During our pre-work workout, a few weeks back, I'd seen her running on the treadmill beside me, fast. Too fast. Panting hard, smacking the track with New Balance-soled feet, her angled elbows swinging wildly, sprinting. Until she wasn't. Having leapt abruptly and landed on the plastic ledges either side of the whizzing track, her torso collapsed against the control panel. After, we'd regrouped as usual outside the changing room. Her composure restored, her still-damp hair appearing a darker blonde. We took the stairs up to the mezzanine floor to caffeinate. Bodies still flushed from the activity.

What compelled Rach to pursue this career? I knew why I did it. Banks – I understood what they were. Ruthless, efficient money-machines with a byproduct of social mobility. Really, what other industry would have offered me the same chance? Unlike my boyfriend, I didn't have the prerequisite connections or money to venture into politics. The financial industry was the only viable route upwards. I'd traded in my life for a sliver of middle-class comfort. For a future. My parents and grandparents had no such opportunities; I felt I could hardly waste mine. Yet, it didn't sit right with me to propagate the same beliefs within a new generation of children. It belied the lack of progress – shaping their aspiration into a uniform and compliant form; their selves into workers who were grateful and industrious and understood their role in society. Who knew the limit to any ascent.

I'd rather say something else. Something better. But of course, without the legitimacy of a flashy title at a blue-chip company, I wouldn't have a platform to say anything at all. Any value my words have in this country is derived from my association with its institutions: universities, banks, government. I can only repeat their words and hope to convey a kind of truth. Perhaps that's a poor justification for my own complicity. My part in convincing children that they, too, must endure. Silence, surely, was the least harmful choice.

Rach had moved on.

'This weekend means big things,' she told me. Serious, exciting things. Things she abstracted to diamond-ring emojis. I wasn't sure that I was ready for any things. I knew these were the things to want, the right things to reach for. But I felt sick of reaching, enduring. Of the ascent.

His parents tolerated me. As good, socially liberal parents would. They were patient with their son in the matter of his relationships. They imagined, I imagined, that this was a phase. Why prolong it with negative attention? And so they accommodated it. Welcomed it – me, ostensibly. In fact, they insisted, he told me more than once, insisted that I join the family for their anniversary celebrations.

I'd met them before, of course. Though nothing like this weekend. It had always been in London, before, four of us around a restaurant table. A two- or three-hour limit on how long we would all be together. The conversation light, and entertaining. They really did know how to entertain. How to talk, to ask, to listen, how to converse. They conjured a sense of occasion. Especially the father, who wielded words with deft precision, like a physical instrument. A scalpel, perhaps, or a quill.

Sitting around a dim-lit table, a few months back, in a windowless restaurant beneath an art gallery, I watched the father speak through lips tinged red with wine (ordered after a wide-ranging and apparently very welcome, vigorous discussion with the sommelier). He raised up his quill and drew me into their world. On the page of that evening I was a part of it, I belonged. Yet, it was a distanced intimacy. Sincere but lacking permanence or consequence beyond a particular interaction. He asked me variations of the same questions each time. With the same indulging interest he extended to the restaurant staff.

The mother's ambivalence was more traditional.

She introduced me once with the awkward mouthful, 'our youngest's latest lady-friend'. Followed by a knowing smile to the acquaintance who had inquired. Still, I understood her. I felt I could see it through her eyes: to a love of her son, yes. But also, the family she had come from and the one she'd married into. Futures and children and purity – not in any crass, racial sense, no. Of course not. It was a purity of lineage, of history: shared cultural mores and sensibilities. The preservation of a way of life, a class, the necessary higher echelon of society. Her son's arrested development (and what was this relationship, if not childish folly?) should not wreck the family name.

I was unsurprised to learn the titles and heritage properties were all on the father's side. There was an uncertainty beneath the mother's hostility that I almost identified with.

In the morning, I watched as their son sat on the edge of his bed and squeezed a sugar-coated tablet from a blister pack. He stared down at the white speck in his hand until finally – with needless, performative resolve – he threw his head back and clasped hand over mouth until all was swallowed. *Citalopram, 5mg. One per day or as directed by your doctor*. He leaned forward, flushed, threw the pack aside. Gulped water from the glass on his bedside table. Then looked over to me, expectant, like he'd just finished all the broccoli on his plate. I was across the room, pinning up my hair. We formed a perfect scene. Sun sliced through the sash windows. His room was bright and sparse and he sat small in it at the edge of the frame, a plump suitcase on the floor beside him. I chuckled and he smiled back, uncertain. I went over to him, cupped his jaw in my left hand and swept the soft edge of his hair back with my right. It was time to go.

He lifted the case into the boot of his car. Cold morning sun lit us unforgivingly and the air smelled damp. But he appeared inflated, revived. Imbued by the outdoors with the promise of a drive in the country, his family, his home, all ahead. Before I left, he placed his hands around my waist and leaned down for a kiss.

'Could I, possibly, steal you away?' he said, eyes smiling.

A part of me did want to get in the car with him and drive off. To spare myself the tense and unhappy day ahead. The full calendar of bullshit meetings, glass cliff-edges, and lying to children. But – to be rash, to act on impulse, to live like him . . . No. Though I had begun to recognize its confines, I remained bound to the life I led. I needed to keep moving. Gently, softly, I guided his arms away. Back to his sides.

I'd see him tonight.

Strategy Onsite

At the onsite, we review the latest figures, the overall trends, the key drivers of those trends, or – perhaps, the steps to determine the key drivers of those trends. I sit with right ankle over left, knees together, shoulders back, arms on the table, hands soft. Prepared. When I speak, I am to-the-point with a measured pace and an even tone. Backed by the data. Illustrated with slides.

Mid-afternoon, there's a comfort break. The men stand, stretch, wander the room. The air is stale from sweat and talk and sandwiches. One man gestures at the espresso machine, says he doesn't know how it works: which button to press, where to put the pod. When is the receptionist coming back? The others concur, they don't know either. They ask me, perhaps I know.

Well.

I make their coffees. And if they'd like, add frothed milk to the top. The men, relieved, say oh, thank you.

Thank you.

After, I wait for Merrick in the small office. It's cordoned off from the open-plan area with glass panes. This place is all glass. Its glass separates and divides without transparency. Still, Lou manages to watch. He watched the PA stop me on the way back to my desk. Watched over monitor tops as I walked across the floor and into the former managing director's former office. And he's watching me now, his neck straining with flagrant nosiness. I place my things – a notebook, pen, wallet – on the desk and sit down.

Let Lou watch.

But it's there. *Dread*. Every day is an opportunity to fuck up. Every decision, every meeting, every report. There's no success, only the temporary aversion of failure. *Dread*. From the buzz and jingle of my alarm until I finally get back to sleep. *Dread*. Weighing cold in my gut, winding up around my oesophagus, seizing my throat. *Dread*. I lie stretched out on the couch or on my bed or just supine on the floor. *Dread*. I repeat the day over, interrogate it for errors or missteps or – anything. *Dread, dread, dread, dread*. Anything at all could be the thing that fucks everything up. I know it. That truth reverberates in my chest, a thumping bass line. *Dread, dread*, it's choking me. *Dread*.

I don't remember when I didn't feel this.

Oh, you're here. Good.

Merrick's face appears huge, beaming with effusive American warmth and insincerity. The conferencing screen refocuses, then pans out, revealing a woman sat beside him.

Good, Merrick says again.

The woman doesn't smile.

I know this woman. My colleagues call her that woman. They say they know how *that* woman got *that* job. They say worse, too. She's a frequent, favourite topic of theirs. This successful woman. This beleaguered, embattled woman. Kicked about and laughed about. Anyway, now she supports other women. She's a regular speaker on the women's events circuit. With fourteen mentees, apparently. And here she is with Merrick. Sitting back, her arms crossed, staring stone-faced down at me.

Well, shit. Ain't I a woman?

Merrick hasn't started yet. He's fidgeting and saying oh um yes well. He places his palms flat on the table, says well, then leans back and adjusts his glasses. Um, yes. He looks from the woman to me.

The unpleasantness is behind us, he finally says. We'd like to put all that behind us and move forward. In a new direction.

He attempts a milky smile.

The woman puts it simply, they want *diversity* now.

Merrick nods with ludicrous gravitas.

Yes, he says. Indeed! Exactly. He drums the table. And that's why he's speaking to me now, he says. Lou's already on board.

They go on:

Joint leadership, says Merrick.

A big opportunity, says the woman.

I'm very lucky, they both agree.

The floor, the tight-packed rows of suited men, oper-
ates with a lurching autonomy. Even after weeks
without *strategic direction* from this glass box. The men
are laughing, breathing, talking in twos or threes,
gathered around a screen. Or standing, chests puffed,
and pointing. Punctuated by an occasional woman.
Some crouch down, their noses in plastic trays of early
dinner or late lunch. There's a stink to it. So many
men talking and sweating and burping and cough-
ing and existing – packed in sleeve to sleeve. Dry,
weathered faces; soft, flabby cheeks; grease-shined
foreheads. Necks bursting from as-yet-unbuttoned
collars. All shades of pink, beige, tan. Fingers stab-
bing at keyboards and meaty fists wrapped around
phone receivers. Or handsfree, gesturing and talking
into slender headsets while tossing and catching a ball
or pen.

Is this it – the crescendo of my career?

My life?

Lou stands, waves. He's heading over, smiling.

Lou!

I grew up dirt poor, you know. Dirt-fucking-poor in a shack, essentially, in Bedford. So, I get it. I get the grind. All this – it's as foreign to me as it is to you. Really. And I respect it, what you're about. The hustle. I do. So, look, of course I agreed to share the promotion. Of course. You deserve this, just as much as me. Okay? Okay. Don't let anyone tell you different. Fuck, I'm excited. For this, for us – the *dream team*! Alright, well. Just wanted to tell you that. Anyway. The boys are heading downstairs for a cheeky one to celebrate.

You coming along?

Back at my desk, I savour the rare moment of quiet. With Lou and the rest out celebrating, I feel an unfamiliar calm in this space. Curiously, I appreciate anew the physicality of my work area. I have the corner window spot. Lou's desk is across from mine. A two-foot-tall felt-padded divider is all that separates us during the thousands of hours we spend here together. The various teams we will now jointly manage occupy the rows of monitors and softly whirring machines surrounding me.

This success, this attainment: everything I've strived for. Within my hands. My fingers tight around a joist of the proverbial ceiling. I have a two-thousand-dollar ergonomic office chair and a Bluetooth headset that flashes, contentedly, from the glossy cube it reclines on to charge. Three thirty-two-inch monitors render red and green with breathtaking intensity. And a stack of business cards; each bearing my name and corporate title – another reprint needed now, on weighty stock beside the bank's embossed logo.

This is everything.

I have everything.

In a panorama around me, the sky is melting: reds and oranges into inky blue and nighttime. I stare through the surely colour-distorting, anti-UV-tinted, floor-to-ceiling window-walls. Out past the skyscrapers and into the blurred green-grey horizon beyond. My fingers feel numb but my face is hot, and prickles. I log out of my workstation, pack up my handbag and head towards the lifts.

Here I Am At The Station, I Should

The departure boards display leisurely. Flick from one of two, to two of two, and back again. I find mine amongst the screens. A platform number shines blurry from a handful of orange dots.

So, here I am at the station. I should go find my platform and get on the train. It's a forty-minute ride. He'll meet me on the other end. Parked outside the station in his Mini, ready to drive me the rest of the way.

I don't feel that I'm going on a journey. Here I am, no heavy bags or comfortable shoes. I'm still dressed for work, I'm here straight from the office. The leather tips of my shoe-boots wink against sharp-pressed hems.

It would have been better to make this trip tomorrow morning.

But I'm here now. And I should at least move. I'm in the way, standing here. Jostled by the currents of rushing people, dawdling people, people arranged as families, clustered like ducklings. I'm right in the throughway. So come on now. Lift left foot and swing it ahead, spring forward. Don't slow down, don't stop. Don't think. Just keep it moving.

Go get on the train.

But here I am,
still
stood, still
at the station.
I really should

21:04
LONDON PADDINGTON [PAD]
TO
NEWBURY [NBY]

When the drinks trolley stops, I buy another minia-ture bottle of non-specific red wine. The train hurtles on. On from London, from the office. Fields and trees, shrubs, parallax past the grubby window.

I'm unsure about this weekend. It seemed fine, even enjoyable, when proposed. Months away, abstract.

But here it is, now, and here I am, too. And this train – very real, very concrete and travelling fast – is tearing us together.

Close your eyes.

•

I remember hospitals as large, confusing, dirty places. Rows of sick beds, separated only by thin track curtains and a charade of privacy. A miserably small shared sink beneath a dim window that looked on to the ward corridor. Trios of bolted-together plastic chairs. Even-ing visiting hours; seeing her there, laying not-quite comfortably. Drips and buttons and tubes. A kitchen-towel-lined tub of grapes on the bedside cabinet. The smell of disinfectant couldn't convince, didn't erase.

But now, for me, it's private rooms. Fresh-cut flowers and espresso.

•

Serious, the doctor labours the word. Tells me I need to take this seriously.

Her blouse is caramel. Her blouse is satin. Its satin swoops out, then in, to the waist of her slacks. My eye is drawn to the bumps and outlines of a lace trim beneath, a cursive M crowning her chest.

Are you listening? she says.

Syrupy light fills her small consultation room. Suspends us both like fossilized insects in amber. She extends a hand towards me, then stops. My own are arranged one over the other, on my lap.

I shake my head, attempt a smile.

Sorry, I say. I'm listening.

I am not sure why I do anything, sometimes. Why do I inhale? Why do I apologize? Or say I'm fine, thanks. And you? Why do I stand back from the platform edge?

These aren't sophisticated or clever questions. But still, sometimes, I can't answer. I can't remember the right answer.

•

Waiting for the Central Line at Liverpool Street, I once saw a man's Blackberry slip up out of his hands, then drop down, comically, on to the tracks. He stood for a moment. Blank. A toddler before the tantrum. Then the eruption – a hot stream of profanity. His face reddened. His satchel flap flopped about and his suit jacket billowed as he thrashed his arms around like a flightless bird. He peered over the platform edge. Leaning, looking, out on to the tracks. Contemplating climbing down? Fuck, he said again. Then ran both hands back through his hair and left the platform.

•

I feel. Of course I do.

I have emotions.

But I try to consider events as if they're happening to someone else. Some other entity. There's the thinking, rationalizing I (me). And the doing, the experiencing, her. I look at her kindly. From a distance. To protect myself, I detach.

•

Recorded delivery? Yes; seven pounds extra; please. Alright, the assistant said from across the Snappy Snaps counter. He grabbed a printed slip and pressed it between his lips as he dropped my passport into a little plastic envelope and sealed it. Then he looked down at the sealed envelope and swore. The forgotten paper parachuted from his mouth, drifting back-and-forth, down to his feet. Buoyed by that small gust of irritation. He tore open the envelope with an exaggerated two-handed motion that stretched the thin, grey

41

plastic to breaking. Out popped a flash of maroon; it met the table with a limp slap.

•

Love. It's a sip of Coke, not that pleasant, sharp on the tongue, but fizzes delightfully from can to mouth to dampening throat. She was speaking, slightly chorused, from the periodically placed televisions around the office floor. Wearing a red suit overexposed to pussy pink, her red lips over-stated her place in women's history. They played it again: The country I love. Her face crumpled like an empty can on *love*, stamped down. She turned away from the podium – so quick. I wanted to hear it again; but she was turning, heading back up to that black door; *love*, again! And the door opened, then closed up around her. Cut, back to the studio.

•

I love you, he said, a timid voice, that first time. After four pints of deniability. Now it's with an everyday, pragmatic brusqueness. Love you! When I leave for work. Love you! Before we hang up. And sometimes also, tongue in cheek, *je t'aime!*

I say it, too, of course. Perhaps that's all it is? The saying of it, and then the acting it out.

•

Unstructured time is unusual for me. Too much think-ing. I don't know what to make of myself. I have my phone, I should catch up on emails. There's always more emails. Merrick's probably firing things over right now. But the train reception is patchy.

And I'd rather sip wine.

•

Back when I bought the flat, the solicitor said I needed a will. After exchange, her colleague in Estates Plan-ning leafed through my binder: statements of assets, accounts, insurance policies – home, health, life. Expressions of wishes. My net worth, at least an attes-tation to it, lay open on his desk.

Well, he said, sitting back. Aren't you a clever girl?

I suppose I can understand his bemusement. Why would he expect me to have such a well-presented stack of printouts and photocopies?

In his playful moods, my boyfriend tells me I've got lots of money. Much more than him. He says I'm the one per cent.

Well, money is one thing. He has wealth. Tied up in assets in trusts and holding companies with compli-cated ownership arrangements. Things he pretends to refuse to understand. Compounded over generations. What's the difference? he asks. I tell him. One of us goes to work at six a.m. each morning. The other sits browsing the papers at the café down the road.

This lawyer, now, my lawyer, in planning my estate, has his colleague, some sort of analyst, produce a cashflow model – future earnings and returns, projected under speculative scenarios. This is a complementary service, included in the estate-planning service, intended as a taster for another service which, the lawyer explains, is quite suitable for a young lady on my financial trajectory.

Wealth management, he smiles.

•

My grandfather brought his drill set. I'd bought two pairs of goggles. He laughed when I held one out for him. We took a photo, both of us dusty and smiling. My new shelves floating behind. He advised on other problems around the flat. My languishing plant – he said to cut the dying palm leaves away. Months later, it's green and thriving.

•

Swish. The doctor leans forward and speaks soft. She says I'm strong, I'm a fighter. Says she can tell. I can't just do nothing, that's – that's suicide. She tells me to be responsible. Think of my family. Make a choice.

Nothing is a choice.

But I don't trust myself to say what I mean, so I just say I'm leaving. It's time to get back to work. I look around for my things, I need to go.

Nothing *is* a choice.

And death is not a no-op. It has side effects. I think of the cashflows: the immediate-death scenario. It's the tallest bar in the chart, a grab at money from years to come. A present valuation of me.

It won't be beautiful – she's warning now – it isn't poetry. It won't be what I imagine. Oh and I do know that, I know but – what do I care of beauty?

Nothing is a *choice*.

And I want it. I reach for my bag, then stand and turn. Unhook my coat from the door. She stands, too. Her face a creasing expression of concern and disapproval.

Listen, she says.

•

The train lurches forward again and I touch a hand to my chest. No incision, no pound of flesh – just a needle, a pinch. That was it. Then, the politely evasive phone call, the follow-up scheduled at my earliest convenience. Now they say an operation, weeks of downtime. Adjuvant therapy, after, possibly, radiation or – chemo, even. *Make a choice*. Untold disruption to my career.

The promotion.

These directives: listen, be quiet, do this, don't do that. When does it end? And where has it got me? More, and more of the same. I am everything they told me to become. Not enough. A physical destruction, now, to match the mental. Dissect, poison, destroy this new malignant part of me. But there's always something else: the next demand, the next criticism. This endless complying, attaining, exceeding – why?

•

I don't know which firm, specifically, the protests were targeting. I was a new grad back then, in crispy Primark shirts and soft M&S trousers. Excited, terrified, eager to work. The guards had cordoned off the building's entrance with metal barriers. I pressed through the crowds; a mass of sandals, blonde dreadlocks and body odour. Their poster boards and voices jeered from all sides. Arms crossed, I kept my head down and walked quick, focused on the ground ahead. Some shouted as I showed my card. Security lifted aside the barrier to let me through.

Their eyes held. They watched me cross the divide and disappear through revolving doors.

•

Let's say: A boy grows up in a country manor. Attends

a private preparatory school. Spends his weekends out in the barn with his father. Together they build a great, stone sundial. The boy, now a young man, achieves two E-grades at A-level, then travels to Jamaica to *teach*. His sun shadows cycle round and round and he himself winds up, up. Up until the boy, an old man now, is right up at the tippity-top of the political system. Buoyed by a wealth he's never had to earn, never worked for. He's never dealt in grubby compromise. And from this vantage, he points a finger – an old finger, the skin translucent, arm outstretched and wavering. He points it at you: The problem.

Always, the problem.

•

The other day, a man called me a fucking n – r. A panhandler at Aldgate, big guy, came up too close, and trapped me – between him and the steep drop down to the tracks. He leaned right into my face and spat out those words. Then, laughing, he just walked away.

You don't owe anything.

I pay my taxes, each year. Any money that was spent on me: education, healthcare, what – roads? I've paid it all back. And then some. Everything now is profit. I am what we've always been to the empire: pure, fucking profit. A natural resource to exploit and exploit, denigrate, and exploit. I don't owe that boy.

Or that man. Or those protestors, or the empire, the motherland, anything at all. I don't owe it my next forty years. I don't owe it my next fucking minute. What else is left to take? This is it, end of the line.

I am done.

·

There's no time in October for more than peanut butter, traffic lights, and *liberated slaves*. It's disorientating, prevents you from forming an identity. Living in a place you're forever told to leave, without knowing, without knowledge. Without history.

After the war, the crumbling empire sent again for her colonial subjects. Not soldiers, this time, but nurses to carry a wavering NHS on their backs. Enoch Powell himself sailed upon Barbados and implored us, come. And so we came and built and mended and nursed; cooked and cleaned. We paid taxes, paid extortionate rent to the few landlords who would take us. We were hated. The National Front chased, burnt, stabbed, eradicated. Churchill set up task forces to get us out. *Keep England White*. Enoch, the once-intrepid recruiter, now warned of bloodied rivers if we didn't leave. New laws were drawn up; our rights revoked.

Yet, some survived. And managed somehow, on meagre wages, to put a little aside. Eventually enough to move wife, husband and child from a rented room in a house shared by five families, to a two-up two-down all of their own. That they owned. And an ethic, a mindset, a drive was established then, that persists now. A relentless, uncompromising pursuit.

·

Transcends race, they say of exceptional, dead black people. As if that relentless overcoming, when taken to the limit, as time stretches on to infinity, itself overcomes even limits, even infinity, even this place.

·

I only know Jamaica from stories. Visiting aunts and uncles, cousins – family. Unwrapping wedges of breadfruit; Julie mangos; fruit cake; a rich buttery pear sliced open, spread on to harddough bread; stories about family, sitting out on a veranda into the night, all together, telling each other other stories. A promise of a welcome, warm, loving family, always, retreating. They all fly back.

I stay here. Their English cousin.

·

I went to school with this boy – haven't seen him since Year Six, but I remember his parents used to make him stand at a desk in their front room to do homework each evening. As soon as he got in. No food, drinks, or bathroom breaks. Just stand there and work. His mother bragged about it at the school gate. He even told me, the way kids tell things sometimes, that he'd wet himself one night, stood there. And his mother made him stay. Wet trousers cooling, sticking to his legs, until all the homework was complete.

He got his scholarship to Haberdashers' Aske's. His well-thumbed brochure boasted a *twenty per cent* Oxbridge acceptance rate.

.

But what it takes to get there isn't what you need once you've arrived.

A difficult realization, and a harder actualization.

I understand what this weekend means. Pulling back the curtain, he's invited me to the chambers beyond. It's not acceptance, not yet. It's just a step further, closer. I must learn to navigate it. Through him, and Rach, I study this cultural capital. I learn what I'm meant to do. How I'm meant to live. What I'm supposed to enjoy. I watch, I emulate. It takes practice. And an understanding of what's out of reach. What I can't pull off.

Born here, parents born here, always lived here – still, never from here. Their culture becomes parody on my body.

.

Sitting here, I feel cramped and prickly. My handbag is stowed above. Coat folded over on my lap. I'm hot and my skin is crawling. I want to be off this train, back in my flat, peeling off these scratching clothes and sliding between cool cotton sheets.

I just want to rest. Stop. Just for a minute.

This kind of thinking leads to undoing. Or else, not doing, which is the slower, more painful approach to coming undone. So much still to do. Yet so much, done, already.

I'm still here, aren't I? Soon, it might be over. Maybe I can stop caring. Stop trying – no, I mustn't be rash, can't close doors just yet. It could take years. Luck. It's just opportunity and preparation.

·

My exam prep was meticulous. It was everything. Morning to night, every hour accounted for in my self-devised schedule. I had an absolute dedication, back then, that I've never since recaptured. No distractions, no lost focus. No idle thoughts. It was a meditation. And after months of that devoted study, I walked once more from the station to the school, across the busy junction. I was ready.

And I saw all: forty years stretching indefinitely, racing along a cobbled and sparkling road. Boats and champagne, flights, panoramic views, the board room, flashing trading screens; flickering lights, the corner office, the dark corner of the members' club; green, sprawling grounds. Clouds streaming like wet-stretched cotton; wool, strung across the sky. A sky blue, and cold. Swish, the windscreen wiper wipes across dry glass and –

A lady is shaking my arm and scream-shouting WHAT IS WRONG WITH YOU? There's a car, at a wrong angle, spanning two lanes, others honking and pedestrians stopping to look. It's all stopped – temporarily, the lady has pulled me back on to the island. Shaking me, still.

I aced the exams.

Premonition or plan? Doesn't matter, I keep chasing.

•

I'm greedy for *a hundred years from now*.

•

This is the boom

and this is the climb, you've twinned it, followed it up. Not euphoric, as you'd imagined. But perhaps it never is, when you're in the thing. It can't

last, though, you know. And so, you put it away, you save. *It rains every day in England!* Here you are, with your accounts and now your accountant, and you put things into bonds, into funds; you pound cost average. And you brace yourself for it. Hold cash in accounts, in a wallet, in a box beneath the bed. Gold – you start to consider. Seriously, something is always coming. Words embossed – into brass, into aluminium, you watch videos of men, pouring fire into buckets; the charred, white-hot remains. Money is just belief, reality is perception, so why not? Stow some there, some everywhere. Be careful, though, and save

you see others – Rach, Lou, they spend. They enjoy it. But is their current lifestyle peak truly a new floor? You don't know. But you can weather an emergency, stress-test yourself, you will not be undone by a small thing. You hope. There's only hope. Hope it's enough to weather any bust until the swing back around when you can grab hold, pull up and start the climb again.

·

The small envelope is government-brown in a pile of white. I open it and find my unsmiling face twice amongst the pages. Name, date of birth, citizenship. I am appalled at my relief and at this sort of relief – thin and substantive only as the paper it's printed on. We've seen now, just as then, the readiness of this government and its enterprising Home Secretary to destroy paper, our records and proof. What is citizenship when you've watched screaming *Go Home* vans crawl your street? When you've heard of the banging, unexpected, always, at the door? When *British*, reduced to paper, is swept aside and trodden over? The passport cover feels smooth and new in my hands. Slip it, away. Into the folder at the back of the bottom dresser drawer.

•

Rach sorts efficiently. *Pack, storage, charity*. The pile on the bed beside me, *pack*, is the largest. Her dresses, knitwear, blouses. Soft fabrics rustle as she places each item down. I breathe the musky-citrus scent. She's already set aside the complementary tools: dedicated brushes, combs, shampoos, sprays. All sorts. Her clothes have complex care requirements, detailed on sewn-in tags.

Moving in together – it might even be good for her career, she says. Her voice is muffled and questioning from within the walk-in wardrobe. More networking opportunities?

She emerges with three dresses – bright, floral, patterned numbers – draped across her arms like limp brides. She sighs and sets them down next to me. Chiffon rolls, delicate and tidal, in the breeze from her open window.

Anyway, we can't put our lives on hold, she says. We have to live.

.

The wives and girlfriends are arranged between us in boy-girl-boy formation. Two are heavily pregnant, smiling out from behind big beach-ball bellies, pink and sweaty in the afternoon sun. Here, around Lou's reclaimed-wood picnic table, I am as much an outsider as at the office. Neither man, nor wife. Unclassified. But my boyfriend is his usual chummy self. Sitting beside me, chatting and asking questions. Laughing with Lou and the rest. He can slot in anywhere. And he brings me, too. My ladder among the snakes.

The next week, back in the office, the husband of one pregnant wife sits across from me. His name isn't on the list. No name, no promotion. He sniffs air in. Cheeks puffed, lips tight and nostrils twitching, he obstinately avoids my eyes until finally, he says:

It's so much easier for you blacks and Hispanics.

He says that's why I was chosen, over qualified guys like him. He says he's not opposed to diversity. He just wants fairness, okay?

Okay? he says again.

Okay?

I am still a few sentences behind. But okay, okay, okay.

·

Explain air.

Convince a sceptic. Prove it's there. Prove what can't be seen.

A breezy brutality cuts you each day – how do you excuse it? Your experience? Sliced flesh. Your hope. Evaporation? You cannot cut through their perception of reality. *Breathe*. At night. It creeps out from under; white square against left breast. Grasps, spreads itself around; your neck, it tightens and squeezes. Wake – gasping, face wet, arms tense, chest (cold), don't look at it; eyes up, the bulbs gleam eerie. It's dark.

In choking, quod erat demonstrandum.

·

The Head of Risk looks a bit ridiculous sat across from me. In a polo shirt with sunglasses pushed back into his tousled hair. Without the sharp-pressed blues and greys and whites of his weekday tailoring, he's just another middle-aged man. His body soft and creasing. Rach is unsmiling, stirring her virgin Mojito with a wilting paper straw. Their dog laps water out of a dish beneath our table. I don't know why the restaurant allows this.

This thing has gone on longer than Rach intended. From flirtation to affair to an uncomfortable, secretive overlap with the wife; the eventual separation; and now their tentative, unspoken merger into shared life. Shared dog. And brunch.

Rach chose. Why can't I?

This is an opportunity, it's my chance. To stop the endless ascent. To leave my family better off. And all else behind. To *transcend*.

Why shouldn't I?

And why must I convince this doctor – or anyone? I've made up my own mind. I want to scream it! My life. My choice. And I've made it. I chose.

·

I look at my coat; the dull lyocell feels soft and expensive in my hands. It fits. It's right for walking into this quiet building on this leafy, architecturally interesting street; upstairs to the high-end reception area and then on through to the sunny consultation room. Across from this well-dressed doctor. I earned this coat and this doctor and this life and now this choice.

She's still talking. Explaining. Telling, telling, telling, telling –

No.

My voice is firm. I say I've made my decision.

·

Be the best. Work harder, work smarter. Exceed every expectation. But also, be invisible, imperceptible. Don't make anyone uncomfortable. Don't inconvenience. Exist in the negative only, the space around. Do not insert yourself into the main narrative. *Go unnoticed. Become the air.*

Open your eyes.

•

Two sisters:

One, four years younger, wants to do everything the elder does. Use the same cutlery, wear the same clothes. Go to the same school, the same university. And now, she's at a firm just down the road. The sisters meet for lunch. The younger is sprinting down that same path and the elder can't stop her, can't hold her back. Can't free her from the endless, crushing pursuit.

•

A buzz. He's at the station already.

Nearly there, I send back.

TRANSCENDENCE
(GARDEN PARTY)

Thank you, he says into the sudden silence of the stopped engine. He looks down at the steering wheel. We're parked on the gravel driveway outside his parents' house. Beyond, across the lawn, a few windows glow orange against the night.

He says he's glad I came. With the biopsy, all that stuff – he pauses and turns to me. In the dim light, I see earnestness in his features. His eyes are dark shadows.

'I'm just happy you're okay,' he says. Then leans over and kisses my cheek.

Outside, it's quiet and oppressively still. The wrought-iron entry gate has slid back into a closed grimace. Miniature lamp posts cast narrow yellow cones, illuminating a path up towards the house. The parents greet us at the door. Helen and George – first names, as they insist – bundle me inside. A radiator-bench hulks against one wall of their wide entryway. They're all smiles, close and welcoming. The mother, Helen, rubs her son's shoulder.

They take me through to a cosy, carpeted side room with a crackling fire. Sit anywhere, they gesture towards the arrangement of sofas and armchairs. I do sit, on the worn floral two-seater beside the fire. The father opens a cabinet and reaches, spidery, into the rows of glasses and bottles. Their son chooses a reading chair opposite me, leans back and crosses his ankles. His body unfurls and twists as he eases into a yawing-stretch, his balled hands pull his arms up and out, ending in a slow and melancholy roar.

'So,' the father begins as he pours. 'Tell me how you ended up in finance. Why aren't you off shaking up change in the Labour Party?' He winks. 'Ushering in a new world order.'

'She's more of a Blairite,' says the son.

'Aha –' The father looks back to me, intrigued, but the mother cuts him off, gently reproachful.

'Politics, at this hour?' She smiles at me.

The father carries on pouring.

'Alright, alright,' he says with warm humour. 'Another topic!'

He replaces the decanter, then sits across from me beside his wife and their son, who's now sprawled out on his chair, drink in hand. I feel too warm, sitting this close to the neatly flickering flames.

'Gas!' the father grins. 'You spotted that? I know, I know it's a cheat.'

He tells me about the fireplace, and the tricky mantel restoration a few years prior. His son chips in. The mother, too. They all talk and I observe. Mostly – I am practised at saying nothing. I listen, react, ask, occasionally. They list some of tomorrow's guests, family friends – political types, of course, but also creatives, academics, lawyers, and so on. A quietly dazzling array.

What am I doing here?

Since stepping on to the train, I've felt this gruesome inevitability. Like I can't turn back. But I'm fascinated, too. I've met Georges before, many, across their various guises, the roles they assume. I have observed and examined and concluded before, but now here I am, seeing one at home. With his wife and son. I don't want to be a part of it. I want to grab at it, grab its face and pull open its mouth, prise its jaws apart and reach down, in, deeper. Touch what's inside.

The son asks about his siblings, will they join us?

'Ellie's upstairs, already,' the mother says. 'It *is* late.'

But the father still has questions. With excited and unwavering eye contact he asks my opinions on everything. Love Island? Cambridge? Knife crime; the BRICS; China's investment in Africa?

The questions sound less like questions than elaborately worded treatises.

'— but we can't very well let it carry on unfettered!' He polishes off his drink, then clinks the empty tumbler down. 'Can we?'

The son lies back with his eyes closed. I am uneasy, too tired for such Socratic conversation.

'Right, how about – oh, yes. This is a good one. Everyone will love this. The royal baby? Meghan Markle? Now that's progress, that's modernization. Inspiring stuff.'

Their son, too, had been excited about the wedding. He'd planned a barbecue, put up Union Jack bunting, bought drinks and mixers and gathered friends over. They watched the BBC's coverage with a smirking, wide-eyed sincerity. To him, and them, it seemed to signify – something. He makes eye contact with me from where he sits, across the fireplace.

Inspirational, I agree.

When we finally do say goodnight, the son insists on an impromptu house tour en route up to his bedroom. He's an enthusiastic guide, opening doors with flourish by their brass knobs. *After you* . . . As we go, he spins unlikely tales about the property's history or just recounts, fondly, his childhood memories. Playing Sardines here or hiding a broken vase over in that chest. The rooms are what I'd imagined: grand architecture dressed down in shabby country chic. Mostly, I am impressed by the corridors; they're spacious – seemingly endless – with elaborate mouldings up where the walls finally give way to ceiling. The patterned carpets are well trodden, but bright and cared for. Perfectly laid along corners, up stairways, and through doors. He stops ahead of me, waiting to show off the library. I'm slow to catch up, stopping to take in the occasional artworks as though I'm at a gallery. It's an eclectic collection; cheerfully framed prints (exhibition posters, classics) and photographs hang alongside serious-looking originals, properly stretched, mounted and framed. Plus a few that I assume were painted by the children themselves.

He says the library was his favourite room, growing up. Though he admits it's more of a large study.

'Just with rather a lot of books!'

A few, he points out, were written by his father. Others, older, pertain to individuals from or aspects relating to his meticulously documented ancestral history. A couple, newer, make reference to the father – if only obliquely. Some are just books.

'My father made a name for himself in this room,' he says. The line sounds rehearsed. His father had started at a conservative think tank, then advised policy makers. Bigger and bigger names, morphing his own into a talisman of shadowy political influence. Who knows how much of it is true? I have no way to verify the father's grandiose anecdotes. Still, those shadows loom over the son. He chases after them. But wouldn't he rather do something else?

'What else is as important as this?' he says. Irritation, or perhaps anger, flashes across his eyes. He leans back against the desk, hugs his arms over his chest. Says: he wishes he could be like me. Take up a soulless City job, make a *metric shit ton* of money. But all this – he waves an obligatory arm at the musty shelves around him – it demands more of him. There's a legacy to uphold. It's a compulsion, he says. He has a compulsion to make his mark on this world! It's been bred into him. He allows himself a sour chuckle at that last quip.

It's late. We should go to bed.

He tells me I'm easy to talk to. That we're honest with each other. He says he loves that about me. Okay, he says. He's going to tell me something. Something honest. Something he's never told anyone. He keeps a – no, not a journal, it's a sort of biography, he's continually writing, crafting it. His story, his life, he's penning it over and over, every day, in his mind. Everything he does, before he does it, he tries it against the pages of that biography. Does it fit, does it meet the standard? Could it sit on these shelves? He needs a yes, or it doesn't happen.

That's how he lives, he says.

I can't see much in the shallow dark of his bedroom. It's strange to have ventured into the place that shaped him years ago. I can make out the blocky silhouette of a bookcase, well stocked and serious from his teenaged reading. A few dim stars glow-in-the-dark against the ceiling.

Beside me, sleeping, he is formless as water. Unperturbed by the day's anxieties. He breathes steadily. With him, I have become more tolerable to the Lous and Merricks of this world. His acceptance of me encourages theirs. His presence vouches for mine, assures them that I'm the right sort of diversity. In turn, I offer him a certain liberal credibility. Negate some of his old-money political baggage. Assure his position left of centre.

I turn my phone to silent. Perhaps he doesn't recognize the pragmatism of our coupling as I do, or Rach would. As his father surely must. But it's there. In his imagined autobiography, this relationship will ultimately reduce to a sentence – maybe two. Thin evidence of his open-mindedness, his knack for cultural bridge-building.

Everything is a trade.

Lou slides on to my screen. The PA's offline, his email says, and we need Monday-morning flights to New York. Merrick wants us at the Americas onsite. I close my eyes – exhale – at the implication. I want to tell him no, tell him to get his own fucking ticket. The screen's rectangular echo remains, luminous against my eyelids. Now isn't the time to be difficult, I know, and I'll have to book my own ticket anyway (inhale).

What's one more? He's included his passport number, expiry date and a smiley-face at the end.

Exhale,

inhale.

Booked, I reply, after. 7.35 a.m. LHR. Boarding pass attached.

I almost start scrolling, down to where I know I'll find my sister's name, with the link she sent me yesterday to some show or other we've both been wanting to see. Instead, I let the screen dim, then flick, to nothing.

Absent my phone's glow, the dark is perfect. My eyes are slow to adjust. The quiet here is absolute. I feel unobserved. Though I know what is to come, and what is expected of me, at tomorrow's party. I understand the function I'm here to perform. There's a promise of enfranchisement and belonging, yes. A narrative peak in the story of my social ascent. Of course, they – the family, even the guests – knew I could not turn down such an invitation.

I will be watched, that's the price of admission. They'll want to see my reactions to their abundance: polite restraint, concealed outrage, and a base, desirous hunger beneath. I must play this part with a veneer of new-millennial-money coolness; serving up savage witticisms alongside the hors d'œuvres. It's a fiction-alization of who I am, but my engagement transforms the fiction into truth. My thoughts, my ideas – even my identity – can only exist as a response to the partygoers' words and actions. Articulated along the perimeter of their form. Reinforcing both their self-hood, and its centrality to mine. How else can they be certain of who they are, and what they aren't? Delineation requires a sharp, black outline.

'That's a pretty dress.'

The mother looks over at me, from across the kitchen. We're awash in sweet light. A wall of bifold French doors accordions open, spilling the kitchen out on to a vast garden and rushing us with crisp morning air. Beyond, four men in nondescript white uniforms inspect spots around the lawn. Metal poles, bundles of white fabric and coiled rope are set out around them. They don't look over.

The mother takes a mug down from a cabinet, and fills it from a gently steaming tea pot. She slides it along the counter towards me.

'Rosemary, from the garden.'

Pinpricks flush my arms as I touch my fingertips to the hot sides of the cup. She details the day's plan. Casual, she emphasizes. A finger buffet, a little music.

'That's the marquee, they're setting up.' She nods towards the men. 'Christine – our caterer – recommended it. Can't trust this weather to hold up!'

She stands a little to my side, still looking out at the garden.

It'll be quite the party.

'Well, we wanted to mark the occasion, yes. Forty years. But really, it's just a good excuse to bring everyone together. Family, friends of the family.' She smiles at me again, with sympathetic brows. Her face is squarish, only finely lined, and softened with a white, peachy fuzz.

'It's lovely to have you with us,' she says.

Opened up like this, the kitchen is big, limitless: the entire garden, the hills beyond, even the pale sky is within reach. The floor is tiled slate, and there's a large island with a hob in the centre. Over on the back wall, oak cabinets display old-fashioned decorative plates and glassware. The son is upstairs still, sleeping. I probably should have stayed up there in the bedroom and read, or just lain beside him, and waited.

'Toast?'

She sets four slices into the machine and clicks it down. Peanut butter, Marmite, jam – she lays the spreads out, placing each on the counter as she names it, next to our mugs. I squint at the handwritten labels on each jam jar, then choose one that looks like apricot. Toast on plates. She's efficient with a blunt knife, working butter thinly across the charred surface. Like a monk refusing to enjoy the ritual, or succumb to any excess. But then she bites, and chews. And her eyes close as if to better taste and smell. I watch her swallow. Then sip tea. Bite again, chew. Swallow.

Everything feels suspended.

The mother, oblivious to this sudden slowing of our time, bites once more. Her jaw grinds rhythmically, bulging and elongating; tendons, emerging taut, flicker up past her ear and into greying wisps of hair. By her temple, a bone or cartilage or some other hard aspect of her bobs and strains against the stretched-white skin. The entire side of her face is engaged in this elaborate mechanical action until, climactically, the soft-hung skin of her neck contracts familiar and the ground-down-mushed-up toast, saliva and butter, worked into a paste, squeezes down; is forced through the pulsing oesophagus, is swallowed.

She lifts the mug to her mouth, and drinks.

Metal drags against metal as the men join poles together, forming abstract outlines. Blunt and earthy: the striking thuds and grunts reverberate as the men tether the structure to grass. The mother purses her lips – oo – as she listens. How long will it take the lawn to recover? From these posts and poles hammered, driven in. And soon the guests; their bodies weighing down on to it, heels puncturing it, as they wander or mill around.

'Ellie will be down soon,' the mother says. 'To give me a hand with all this.'

She waves at the busying scene in front of us. A few other people, catering staff I guess, carry boxes or chairs or bundles of long-stemmed flowers over from somewhere left of view.

'Oh, no,' she says, when I offer to help. 'Ellie's coming.'

She dusts the crumbs from her hand on to the empty plate and tells me about a friend of her son's, something of an old flame, actually. All that is ancient history, she assures me. I'm not to worry. Still, she says, this friend often pops by early on these occasions, to lend a hand.

'I'm positively overrun with helpers.' She makes a gesture of mock exasperation.

I mirror the mother's amusement, recognizing her practised enunciation; how deliberately she forms consonants around laboured vowels. She is wholly illuminated, in this moment, here, in her stunning kitchen. Then she clears the plates, and we return to our performance of host and guest. We make small talk, absently, until I hear at last the warbling approach of the baby with Ellie, as promised. Ellie responds matter-of-factly to the baby's ambiguous noises, as though they're engaged in a real, and tiresome, conversation. Brisk – she finger-waves a greeting to me, then mother and daughter huddle to talk logistics. Where the cars will park, what time the band will arrive – things I assume must have been considered already and agreed weeks prior. The baby reaches out to me, fussing, leaning over and wriggling out of the daughter's arms. She parks him in a highchair – a stylish, walnut contraption. He kicks, then swings, his little feet. Again, his hands reach out towards me.

It feels like a touch from the mother, her gaze cloying and silky as spiderwebs against my skin. I turn to look at both, mother and daughter. The elder's face stretches into another smile.

'All this party talk,' she says, 'you must be bored senseless.' Before I can answer, she points me to the solution: a garden stroll.

'Fresh air is so invigorating,' she says.

So I cross the kitchen and pass through, out into the garden, careful not to disturb the staff arranging tables and decorations. The lawn extends in all directions into geometric eruptions of flowers and leafy plants. Further back, stone steps lead down to a mossy fountain, framed by hedges and still more flowers. It's all beautifully cultivated, with just a touch of overgrown wildness. Presumably achieved via attentive gardening. I look back at the house, up at the sweeping, creeping ivy grandeur. It's a mansion, really. Toad of Toad Hall – my embarrassingly childish frame of reference surprises me. But it's true, this place looks like the delicate, sprawling watercolour illustrations I remember from childhood. And somehow I've stepped into it. Here I am, on the inside.

Ey-hey. Pretty lay-day.

One of the labourers, carrying a large folded table under his arm, calls out from a few metres away. When I look over, he stops walking, sets the table down and leans against it.

Pretty lady, you think it's fair? You stroll in the sunshine while I work, eh? What a world!

His sing-song voice rings sour. He's older – maybe late forties. Damp hair sticks flat to his brow even as he shakes his head.

I wonder, who else in this household would he say that to? In his preferred social hierarchy, his understanding of *fair*, who is allowed to walk, to breathe, to enjoy a Saturday? He has bluish bags beneath his eyes and pronounced jowls. His entire body slumps as he stands there, waiting for his answer. He disgusts me, I realize. His impotent anger, his need to assert himself – to tell me who he thinks this world belongs to. I turn away, and start towards the steps at the back of the garden.

Pretty lady? he calls after me. *Joking*, pretty lady come back!

I keep going until I no longer hear his laughter.

It's cooler by the fountain. A few fat, silvery-orange fish loop around the pond beneath. I watch them dart between rocks, disappearing and reappearing, glinting in the rainbow refracted light. *Convince the lowest white man* . . . LBJ had accurately diagnosed the importance of a coloured other to placate his people. I've watched with dispassionate curiosity as this continent hacks away at itself: confused, lost, sick with nostalgia for those imperialist glory days – when the *them* had been so clearly defined! It's evident now, obvious in retrospect as the proof of root-two's irrationality, that these world superpowers are neither infallible, nor superior. They're nothing, not without a brutally enforced relativity. An organized, systematic brutality that their soft and sagging children can scarcely stomach – won't even acknowledge. Yet cling to as truth. There was never any absolute, no decree from God. Just viscous, random chance. And then, compounding.[1]

I let myself out, lifting and replacing the rusted lever to lock the fence behind me. Even from the periphery, just here, the house seems already quite far. I am not much of a rambler, but right now I want to walk. Further than even their ample garden will allow. I want distance. I think. Up through the hills.

I walk to it.

1. It is remarkable, even
   in the ostensible privacy of my own thoughts
   I feel
   (still)
   compelled
   to restrict what I say.

It spreads, the doctor said when I asked her how it's killing me. She explained the stages. Said if I leave it too long, let it spread too far, the damage will be unsurvivable. Metastasis: it spreads through the blood to other organs, growing uncontrollably, overwhelming the body.

There is a basic physicality to the family's wealth. The house, these grounds, the staff, art – all things they can touch, inhabit, live on. And the family genealogy; all the documents, photographs. Books! A curated history. I press my palm against the rough bark of a tree trunk and look up at its branches. Cool and leafy, the air here tastes like possibility. Imagine growing up amongst this. The son, of course, insists the *best things* in life are free. All this was, is, free to him. The schoolchildren here don't need artificial inspiration from people like me. They take chances, pursue dreams, risk climbing out to the highest, furthest limb. They reach out – knowing the ground beneath is soil, soft grass and dandelions.

I can even understand Lou, considering all this. The underdog he sees in himself, believing in his own fairytale of *overcoming*; from Bedford to midway up the corporate ladder with a two-bed two-bath in a W9 postcode. Lou will make it, I expect. He'll have all this. He'll upsize, then upsize again, soon enough. Get the kids on waiting lists for the right schools. Schmooze up to the right people, get that next promotion, the ski invite, start buying better suits. He'll evolve. Until he slips in, indistinguishable. His children will grow up knowing only this. Believing it's free.

The answer: assimilation. Always, the pressure is there. *Assimilate, assimilate* . . . Dissolve yourself into the melting pot. And then flow out, pour into the mould. Bend your bones until they splinter and crack and you fit. Force yourself into their form. *Assimilate*, they say it, encouraging. Then frowning. Then again and again. And always there, quiet, beneath the urging language of tolerance and cohesion – disappear! Melt into London's multicultural soup. Not like Lou. Not here. Not into this.

I have lived life by the principle that when I face a problem, I must work to find an action I can take to overcome it; or accommodate it; or forge a new path around it; excavate the ground beneath it, even. This is how I've been prepared. This is how we prepare ourselves, teach our children to approach this place of

78

obstacle after obstacle. *Work twice as hard. Be twice as good.* And always, assimilate.

Because they watch (us). They're taught how to, from school. They are taught to view our bodies (selves) as objects. They learn an MEDC/LEDC divide as geography – unquestionable as mountains, oceans and other natural phenomena. Without whys or wherefores, or the ruthless arrows of European imperialism tearing across the world map. At its most fundamental: the nameless, faceless, unidentified (black) bodies, displayed, packed, and chained, side-by-side head-to-toe, into an inky-illustrated ship. Conditions unfit for animals. In perpetuity, they're shown these pictures, over and over in classrooms again. Until it becomes axiom; that continuous line from object,

     to us.

And then, they look:

Fig 1.

    He's not shy about it. He stands there, legs
    apart, in rubber-soled shoes and a cheap suit.
    Watching. Just two metres away. His eyes,

expectant, hold on to your body, his fingertips tap at a two-way radio. The deafening static of his suspicion builds as he trails you through the aisles. He stays a few strides behind you, wherever you go. Your movements are calm and deliberate, but you feel your pulse pound in your neck. You should look right at him. Confront him. Demand a reason, at least. But you can't.

You know you can't.

A buzzing in your bag startles you. You hesitate, nearly ignore it. But then pull yourself together. Say, *come on*, and fish the phone out from your bag. Feel the crackle of his attention down your neck and along your arm, through your palm and into your fingers as they fold around smooth plastic and your thumb slides up.

Hello? says a disembodied voice.

He's watching, watching watching.

Fig 2.

Outside the corner shop, over the road from your secondary school, there's often a queue of girls waiting. A shop assistant – turned bouncer for the after-school rush – stood at the door. Two at a time, get in line, one-in-one-out, he intoned, as if reciting from a holy text. But then he'd wave in two or three girls who hadn't bothered with the queue. Schoolgirls with cherry'd lips, clumpy black eyelashes, and blonde hair that fell in limp curls about their shoulders, he waved them in. Then he glared at the queue, told it to keep the noise down.

Fig 3.

New York Sunday night, London Saturday morning. You fly the round trip regularly for work. But the attendant stops you. At Heathrow, Sunday afternoon, the attendant lunges into your path before you can reach the business desk. Places a firm hand against your upper arm. The attendant's fingers – who knows what else they've touched? – now press into the soft, grey wool of your coat. You look down at this hand on your body; at the flecks of dirt beneath its fingernails, the pale hairs sprouting from its clammy skin. And then its owner, the attendant, points and speaks loudly, as though you won't understand, says: Regular check-in is over there.

The attendant won't acknowledge your ticket, no, just waves you over to the long queue. It winds back and forth, penned in between ropes, all the way to the regular check-in desk. The attendant says: Yes, there's your line, over there.

Fig 4.

Walking from the library back to college one evening, you spot them huddled on the bridge. Faces lit sickly-green by their phones. A couple have bikes, one girl leans over the side, spitting into the river below. Talking slows, as you approach, they twist and turn their attention towards

you keep your pace. Left foot, then right. Keep your head down, keep going. There is no back, or even forwards; realize this. There's only through it, endlessly, treading it. This hostile environment. This hostile life. And then, that word – that close-sesame word that imbues even *kids* on a bridge with the wealth and stature of this great, British empire; its

architecture, its walls, statues loom magnif-
icent on every side – that word the spitting
girl spits at you, before spraying more saliva
through her teeth. Rips into silence, not
water, this time

they're laughing and you're past them
and you don't look back, you just keep going,
and ignore behind you the winding kick-spun
sound of pedals spinning fast on their bikes

don't look

The doctor said I didn't understand —

I recall Lou, eating lunch at his desk while Philando
Castile's death played out between paragraphs on his
screen. He held his burrito up above his mouth and
caught falling beans with his tongue as he peeled the
foil back from soft tortilla. The doctor had said I didn't
understand, that I didn't know the pain of it; of cancer
left untreated. I'd wish I'd acted sooner, she said. Pain,
I repeat. Malignant intent. Assimilation – radiation,
rays. Flesh consumed, ravaged by cannibalizing eyes.
Video, and burrito, finished. Lou's sticky hand cupped
the mouse and clicked away.

(understand: the desire is to consume your suffering,

entertain themselves with the chill of it, the hair-on-edge frisson of it; of suffering that reasserts all they know as higher truth / jolts and thrills and scratches the throat as they swallow it whole / that same satisfaction of a thread pulled, of pulling, unravelling, coming undone)

In walking, the crunch and rustle underfoot has yielded to dusty whispers; weightlessness, soft treading. I am lost both literally and in the larger, abstract sense of this narrative. Though looking back, down, I still see the house: red brick towering high behind a white marquee. It seems the house and the marquee and the distance are the only things here now at all. Why am I doing this? I've reduced the son, the family and their home, to choice moments, flashes, summaries. Stitched them together from the words and actions of others. Of people, real and complex individuals. *Transcendence*. I am lifting them up here with me, to these as-yet-unconquered metaphoric planes. Where we can play-act who we are to one another on simplified terms. Which is to say, I am thinking. The mother is right, the air invigorates.

Still, I remain physically here. And I do not feel safe. My presence unsettles colleagues, strangers, acquaintances, even friends. Yes, I've felt the spray of my co-worker's indignation as he speak-shouts his thoughts re affirmative action. *Fucking quotas*. Even Rach, her soft hand on my shoulder as she says she understands, of course. She understands, but it's still tough, you know? It's like being a woman isn't enough any more.

The unquestioned assumption is of something given; something unearned, *taken*, from a deserving and hardworking –

Though these hills are empty, and I am free to walk them, there's the ever-present threat of that same impulse. To protect this place from me. At any moment, any of them could appear, could demand to know who I am, what I'm doing.

Who told me I could do that here?

The son – he loves the stories of monstrous men doing hideous things in glossy offices and Michelin restaurants. He takes voyeuristic delight in the pain and righteous struggle, before the eventual overcoming. Afterwards, he smiles and squeezes my hand, he sits easy. Assured by his participation in the quiet, the happy ending. The solution.

He introduces me to his political friends from across the spectrum. Conservatives who oo and ah and nod, telling me I'm just what this country is about. And so articulate! Frowning liberals who put it simply: my immoral career is counterproductive to my own community. Can I see that? My primary issue is *poverty*, not race. Their earnest faces tilt to assess my comprehension, my understanding of my role in this society. They conjure metaphors of boats and tides and rising waves of fairness. Not reparations – no, even socialism doesn't stretch that far. Though some do propose a rather capitalistic trickle-down from Britain to her lagging Commonwealth friends. Through *economic* generosity: trade and strong relations! Global leadership. The centrists nod. The son nods, too. Now that, they can all agree to.

They take their modern burden seriously; over Beyond Meat burgers with thick-cut chips drizzled in truffle oil.

Per bell hooks: *We must engage decolonization as a critical practice if we are to have meaningful chances of survival* . . . yes, yes! But I don't know how. How do we examine the legacy of colonization when the basic facts of its construction are disputed in the minds of its beneficiaries? Even that which wasn't burnt in the 60s – by

British officials during the government-sanctioned frenzy of mass document destruction. Operation Legacy, to spare the Queen embarrassment. The more insidious act, though less sensational, proved to have the greatest impact: a deliberate exclusion and obfuscation within the country's national curriculum. Through this, more than records were destroyed. The erasure itself was erased.

With breathtaking ease, the facts of Britain's non-war twentieth-century history have been unrooted, dug out from the country's collective memory. Supplanted. Vague fairytales of benevolent imperial rule bloom instead. How can we engage, discuss, even think through a post-colonial lens, when there's no shared base of knowledge? When even the simplest accounting of events – as preserved in the country's own archives – wobbles suspect as tin-foil-hat conspiracies in the minds of its educated citizens?

When I am in the schools, I could try to say something. To the assembly halls of children seeking inspiration. Because even today, the mother country hasn't loosened her grip. Britain continues to own, exploit and profit from land taken during its twentieth-century exploits. Burning our futures to fuel its voracious economy. Under threat of monetary violence. Lecturing us, all the while, about self-sufficiency. Interfering in our politics, our democracies, our access to the global economic stage; creating LEDCs.

Best case: those children grow up, *assimilate*, get jobs and pour money into a government that forever tells them they are not British. This is not home.

Should I say that?

No, I can't charge at it head on. There are conventions, the son says. Familiar, palatable forms. To foster understanding. That's how they do it in speeches, he says. (He sometimes writes political speeches.) Sugarcoat the rhetoric, embed the politics within a story; make it relatable, personal. Honest, he says. Shape my truth into a narrative arc –

Alright, I try it. I tell a story. But he demands more. He wants to know who did what, specifically, and to whom. How did it feel? (Give him visceral physicality.) Who is to blame? (A single, flawed individual. Not a system or society or the complicity of an undistinguished majority in maintaining the status quo . . .) And what does it teach us? How will our heroine transcend her victimhood? Tell him more, he encourages. He says he's listening. He wants to know.

What else could I say – how much detail is enough? Enough to unlock thoughts or understanding or even something basic, human, empathetic within him. It's just not there. Or, I can't speak to it. My only tool of expression is the language of this place. Its bias and assumptions permeate all reason I could construct from it.

These words, symbols arranged on the page (itself a pure, unblemished vehicle for objective elucidation of thought), these basic units of civilization – how could they harbour ill intent?

Fig 5.

white

having no hue due to the reflection of all or
almost all incident light

           black

          without light; completely dark

        without hope or alleviation; gloomy

            very dirty or soiled

bloodless or pale, as from pain,
emotion, etc

benevolent or without malicious intent

              angry or resentful

colourless or transparent

          dealing with the unpleasant
        realities of life, esp in a pessimistic
            or macabre manner

capped with or accompanied by snow

counterrevolutionary, very conservative,
or royalist

                    causing, resulting from, or showing
                                great misfortune

blank, as an unprinted area of a page

                                wicked or harmful

honourable or generous

                        causing or deserving dishonour
                                or censure

morally unblemished

                                (of the face) purple,
                                as from suffocation

(of times, seasons, etc) auspicious;
favourable

bleed white

whiter than white

How can I use such a language to examine the society it reinforces? The society that conceived it; spoke it into existence and fostered it to maturity as its people scribbled cursive enlightenment anywhere I might call home?

The white hand printed on the white van brandishes silvery cuffs against a black backdrop, beside large stamp-effect typeface searing the playground-familiar taunt into taxpayer-funded legitimacy: GO HOME or face arrest.

Fig 6.

> @hmtreasury:
> Here's today's surprising #FridayFact. Millions of you helped end the slave trade through your taxes.

(Her Majesty's Treasury's Twitter account accompanies this cutesy misrepresentation of history with an illustration depicting people, enslaved – including a mother, baby strapped to her back and chain heavy around her neck. The caption boasts of Britain's generosity in *buying freedom for all slaves in the empire.*

Compensating slave-owners for property lost. Did you know?)

Is it true that his family's wealth today was funded in part by that bought freedom; the loan my taxes paid off? Yes. And he is an individual and I am an individual and neither of us were there, were responsible for the actions of our historical selves? Yes. Yet, he lives off the capital returns, while I work to pay off the interest? Yes. But, here I am now, walking through the fruits of it; land he owns, history he cherishes; the familiar grounding, soil, bricks and trees stretching metres high; the sense of belonging, of safety, of being home. He has that here, always, to return to? Yes. Sleeping this morning, did he look renewed? Yes. Yes, of course. He is home.

I didn't show him the flat right away. I'd been reluctant to share this part of me that, while external, felt so personal.

'Is it that one? No, not that one?' he'd teased, pointing at the ugliest buildings we passed as I walked him to it, a few days after completion. He paced around the front garden, while I searched the bunch for a key to the outer door. He rushed up both flights of stairs with lunging, two-step leaps. Inside, the rooms were stripped – only curtains, carpets and a sour musk remained from the previous inhabitants. He ran his hand along the cracked magnolia paint, then crouched to inspect the sealed fireplace. At the far end of the room, he yanked back the curtains and peered out through the big bay windows, rattling in their rotting-wood frames.

'It's rather nice, isn't it?' he said into the glass.

Between my clasped palms, the keys pressed unfamiliar.

'Now,' he said. 'You just need art!'

But first, renovation. The original features are carefully restored. We browse for furniture and decorations. The selected piece arrives via courier in a smart box, along with a crisp white envelope bearing a document titled: Certificate of Authenticity. Also in the box is a folded leaflet printed with *supplemental information about this lithograph*.

When alone for an evening, in this tasteful home I've fashioned, I strip off the day's clothes. Layers, fabric, peel from skin until there's nothing left beneath. Still, nothing more is revealed; no hidden self, no naked-ness. No exotic, exposed other.

Nothing.

I sink into it.

Pull at it, take these strands, gather them up and spool them around you; reconstruct yourself from the scraps. Say: I love you. I love working here. I loved speaking today. No, no it was nothing. I am fine, I am; I'm excited, yes, for the future – say whatever they tell you to say or not say, just survive it; march on into the inevitable. As our mothers, and fathers, did. Our grandparents before them. Survive.

I'm not sure I understood that I could stop, before this. That there was any alternative to survivable. But in my metastasis, I find possibility. I must engage the question seriously: why live? Why subject myself fur-ther to their reductive gaze? To this *crushing objecthood*. Why endure my own dehumanization? I have the flat, savings and some investments, pensions, plus a sub-stantial life-insurance policy. I have amassed a new opportunity, something to pass on. Forwards. To my sister. A fighting chance. Though, she would not want this. Yes, I am leaving her here alone.

But to carry on, now that I have a choice, is to choose complicity.

Surviving makes me a participant in their narrative. Succeed or fail, my existence only reinforces this construct. I reject it. I reject these options. I reject this life. Yes, I understand the pain. The pain is transformational – transcendent – the undoing of construction. A return, mercifully, to dust.

I've walked quite far, I realize.

I turn back to survey the view. Even up here, I feel it against my skin, the thumping nationalism of this place. I am the stretched-taut membrane of a drum, against which their identity beats. I cannot escape its rhythm. Everything awaits, Monday – New York, then back in the office. For the rest of my life these Mondays loom loud, thudding and crushing, crescendoing on to me, tearing through –

– but it's quiet, now. I sit on the grass and look out over the family's bustling estate. The tableau before me moves small and detached from sound, though well-composed. The house and the greenery set a splendid backdrop for the lively garden scene. Fruits and bottles, ripe, laid out, ready for uncorking and consumption; opening mouths. Four figures – dressed in black – erect stands formed of the tiniest strokes, then open up cases. The satisfying *pop*, after the click, the final creak are unheard – but I can almost smell the sweet resin as they, with maternal care, lift instrumental bodies from velvet lining.

There's much here to delight an eagle-eyed viewer. Spot the animated figures: the caterer, clipboard in hand, at the corner smoothing a tablecloth. A loose edge of the marquee flapping harmlessly above – a tiny strand (imagined? hinted?) waving in the welcome breeze. The busy mother pausing to rearrange a table bouquet. The daughter, bouncing an infant, inspecting a bottle, turning to her husband.

Yes, I'm staring, but I do not diminish; I cannot snuff out such vibrancy with my dim view from afar. Still, I have looked – I've seen, and even if I cannot express what it is I saw here, what I've come to understand, I know it's enough.

I've seen enough.

I watch now with the benevolent patience my decision, my untethering from this life, affords. As the son, my boyfriend, walks out through the gate, and takes a shorter path up through these hills. Occasionally obscured by trees, he presses on until he's too large for the scene, stepping out of it, into life. He advances.

'There you are,' he says when he gets to me. 'Hiding out?'

I squint up at his face. He holds up an open bottle of champagne with a roguish grin.

'Pinched some provisions!'

He crouches, then stretches out, until he's lying awkwardly beside me. He sets the bottle down on the grass. His shirtsleeves and collar scrunch out from under his gilet. I think I hear the faint resonance of the band warming up, blending bittersweet into the chirping and rustling soundscape of this place.

'Look. About that puppy business, before –' He stops. I watch him roll on to his back.

'I've been thinking,' he says up to the sky, 'about all this. You know, your – our brush with *cancer*.' He stage-whispers the word. Imbues it with a perverse, buzzing electricity. 'Coming so close to – well, death.

It's given me perspective. A reminder. Of what's important, what truly matters.

'Life, it's . . .' He smiles, and familiar lines crinkle from the corners of his eyes.

'We've got to seize it!'

I can't see London from here. Nothing scrapes or pierces the soft blue sky. And he's better for it. Something about the city, its construction, the industry, the bustling globalization – erodes him. He turns to me, his eyes wide, and searching. He touches his hand to my arm.

'My parents think you're great.' He smiles. We lie in silence, for a moment.

'Fuck it,' he says. 'Let's get married.'

He inches towards me, eyes soft-closed and lips squeezed into a kissy pout. He believes his words in this moment, I believe that. But his is the fleeting belief of a moment, and it will pass. As soon as new fancy strikes, the next adventure. I understand. It's the impulse of a boy who himself understands, in his flesh and bones and blood and skin, that he was born to helm this great nation – upon which the sun has never set. Not yet. It's bright, now. And the sky is impossibly blue. He's himself again. Here. At home, and rendered in sharp contrast to me. But without this place, without that contrast –

What had you hoped to find here?

I should meet his kiss. Then we'll clamber up, brush off, and walk back down to the house holding hands. Guests will be here soon, it's almost time. Everything's coming together. The champagne's tilted over, its fizzy contents puddling on to dry soil and grass. His lips tremble with the strain of pursing; confident in the assumed yes, and yet, uncertain.

Suddenly, so uncertain.

Acknowledgements

Thank you to my editor, Hermione Thompson, and my agent, Emma Paterson, for the insight, support and guidance. Along with Jean Garnett and Monica MacSwan, I couldn't have hoped to work with a better team.

I am grateful to Spread The Word for selecting me for a 2019 London Writers Award. Thank you Bobby, Eva, Ruth and team for the opportunity.

Thanks also to Jackee and Elise Brown, Amina Begum, Harald Carlens, Maja Waite, Han Smith, Niroshini S., Adam Zmith, Salma Ibrahim, Taranjit Mander, Vanessa Dreme, Chloe Davies, Sarah Day, Francisca Monteiro, Lisa Baker, Laura Otal, Anna Hall, Jacinta Read, Katy Darby, Rose Tomaszewska and Sam Copeland.

And to my family – thank you for everything. This book would not have been possible without your support.

Notes

p.v Chapter 4 of Ecclesiastes, NIV translation.

p.75 Lyndon B. Johnson, as quoted by Bill Moyers in a *Washington Post* article, 13 November 1988.

p.86 See *Postmodern Blackness* by bell hooks.

p.90–91 *Collins English Dictionary*.

p.92 HM Treasury account on Twitter, 9 February 2018, since deleted.

p.93 See *Citizen: An American Lyric* by Claudia Rankine for more on the historical self.